Grasshoppers and Crickets

Rose Inserra

Contents

What Are Grasshoppers and Crickets?

Grasshoppers and crickets are insects.
Many grasshoppers and crickets can jump.
Some have wings and can fly.

a grasshopper jumping

a grasshopper flying

Most grasshoppers and crickets
have large back legs,
which they use for jumping.
They can also make sounds
by rubbing together parts of their bodies.
This is known as singing, or chirping.

a cricket

Like all insects, grasshoppers and crickets have a head, a thorax and an abdomen. Most grasshoppers and crickets have two **antennae** (say: *an-ten-ee)*, four wings and six legs.

Grasshoppers and crickets have two large eyes, and three smaller eyes.

The two large eyes are **compound eyes**. Each compound eye has hundreds of tiny **lenses** inside it. The lenses help grasshoppers and crickets to see moving things.

The three small eyes help the insects to see light and dark.

This photo shows the head of a grasshopper.

Differences Between Grasshoppers and Crickets

Grasshoppers	Crickets
 antennae thorax wings head abdomen	 antennae thorax wings head abdomen
short antennae	long antennae
hearing parts on the abdomen	hearing parts on the front legs
active mostly during the day	active mostly during the night
plant eaters	plant and meat eaters
They rub their back legs with their front wings to make a sound.	They rub their front wings together to make a sound.

The Life Cycle of Grasshoppers and Crickets

The life cycle of a grasshopper and a cricket has three **stages**: egg, nymph and adult.

The eggs hatch into nymphs, which look like small adult insects without wings. Nymphs moult, or lose the outer covering on their bodies, many times as they grow to be adults.

This change from an egg to an adult is called metamorphosis (say: *met-a-mor-fa-sis*).

Birds, beetles, rodents, reptiles and spiders eat grasshoppers.

The Life Cycle of a Cricket

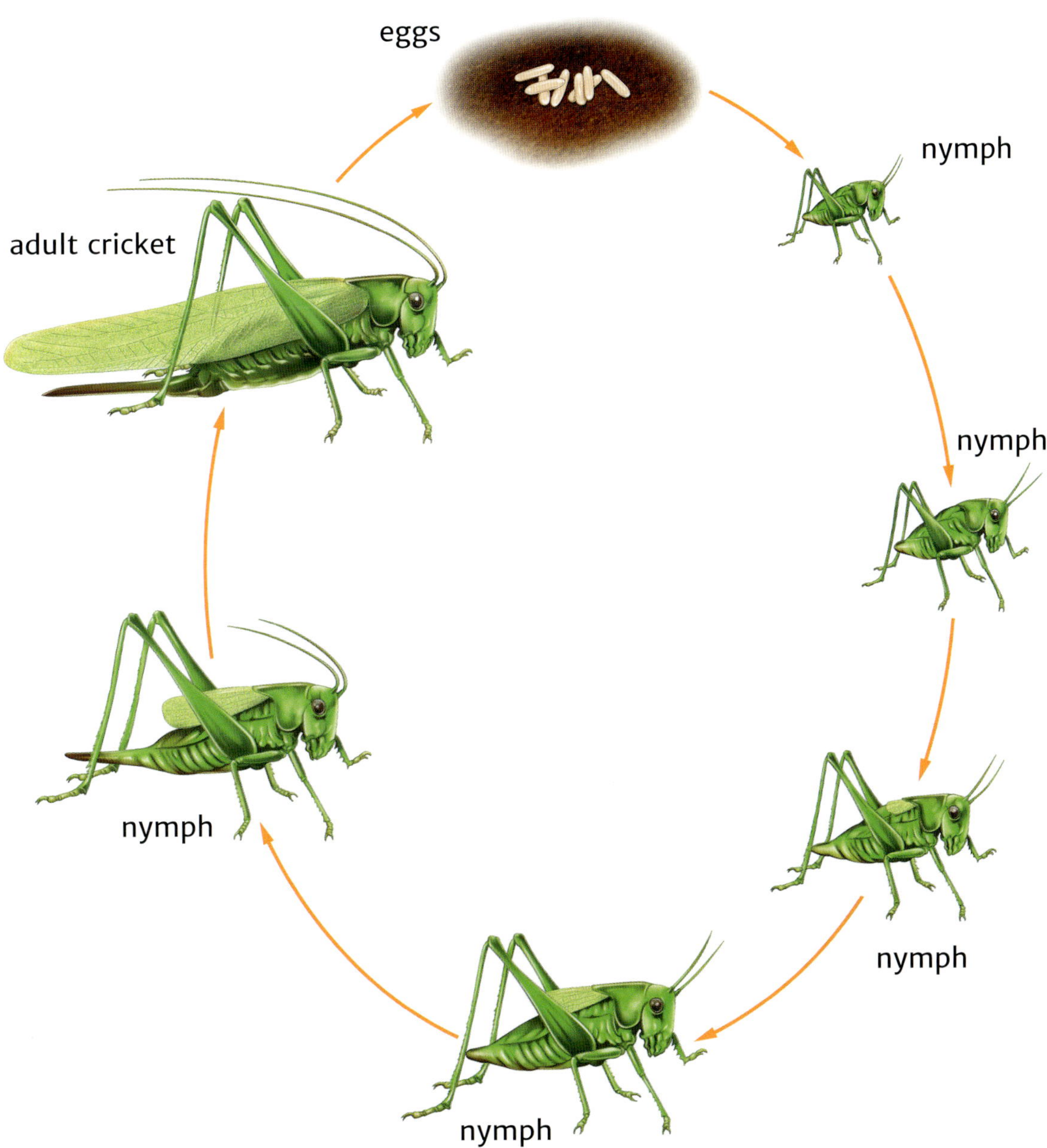

Where Grasshoppers and Crickets Live

Most grasshoppers live close to the ground. There, they can easily find grasses and plants to feed on.

Grasshoppers are most active during the day, but they also feed at night.

Grasshoppers are hard to see in the grass and plants. Their **camouflage** helps them to hide from birds and other animals.

Many crickets live in burrows, in logs or under leaf litter during the day.

Crickets are active at night. This is often the time when they make chirping noises.

A cricket comes out of its burrow in the evening.

What Grasshoppers and Crickets Eat

Grasshoppers eat grasses, weeds, leaves,
flowers and seeds.
Some also eat farmers' crops,
like grains, corn and cotton.

Some grasshoppers eat poisonous plants.
They store the poison in their bodies
so predators will not find them tasty to eat.

A grasshopper eats a leaf.

Crickets eat rotting plants, leaves, moss and fruit. Some crickets also eat other insects and small animals like lizards.

Some crickets crawl into people's houses. When they are inside, they can chew up papers and even make holes in clothes and curtains!

Crickets eat a slice of fruit.

Flying and Singing

Some grasshoppers have very good flying skills.

A locust is a kind of grasshopper that can fly long distances to find food. Sometimes, locusts fly together in a large group called a "swarm".

A swarm of locusts can destroy whole fields of crops by eating them.

Some locusts can eat their body weight in plants each day.

A swarm of locusts flies over a field.

Crickets have special ways of making sounds,
or chirping.
Most rub their wings together quickly.

When a cricket is heard chirping,
it is almost always a male calling for a female.
Sometimes male crickets chirp
to keep other male crickets away.

A male cricket chirps to call a mate.

Most crickets chirp at night, during the warm weather. They chirp faster when the temperature is hotter and slower when it is colder.

Bell crickets are famous for their singing.

Hundreds of years ago, people in Japan used to go to special places where they could listen to crickets chirping and singing.

Special Kinds of Grasshoppers and Crickets

Katydids

Katydids are insects that are related to both grasshoppers and crickets.
They live mostly in trees and bushes.

Their bodies can be shaped like a leaf or a twig.
This camouflage helps to keep them safe from predators.

A katydid can be shaped like a leaf.

The katydid gets its name from the sound it makes when it chirps by rubbing its wings together. People thought this chirping sounded like the words: "Katy did, Katy didn't".

The katydid uses its song to **attract** a mate and tell others where it lives.

A katydid rubs its wings together to sing.

Jerusalem Crickets

Jerusalem crickets are insects that look like giant ants.
They live in dry, sandy places like Mexico and the western part of the USA.

Jerusalem crickets burrow into the soil
to find food.

Jerusalem crickets have different ways
of scaring predators away.
They can bite, and they can make a bad smell.
They can also make a hissing sound
by rubbing a back leg
along the side of their abdomen.

Grasshoppers and Crickets in the Environment

Grasshoppers and crickets help to keep the environment clean. Crickets eat the bodies of dead animals. Grasshoppers and crickets are also food for spiders, birds and lizards.

But some grasshoppers and crickets can be a pest. Large swarms can eat everything in a field and leave nothing behind.

An owl eats a grasshopper.

In some places around the world, grasshoppers and crickets have been part of people's diets for thousands of years.

Grasshoppers and crickets are very high in **protein**, so they are a healthy food to eat.

Farming grasshoppers and crickets for food does not use up a lot of land, water or **energy**, so it is good for the environment.

In Indonesia, grasshoppers are fried with special spices and eaten.

Grasshoppers and crickets are special insects.
Many of them can jump high
and chirp and sing loudly.

Grasshoppers and crickets
help to keep the environment healthy.
They are an important food for other animals
and for many people around the world.

Glossary

antennae (*noun*)	feelers or stalks on an insect's head
attract (*verb*)	to draw interest or attention
camouflage (*noun*)	colours or patterns that help an animal blend into a background
compound eyes (*noun*)	eyes that are made up of different parts that work separately
energy (*noun*)	the power to do work or run machines
lenses (*noun*)	rounded parts of an eye that help an insect or other animal to see
protein (*noun*)	something that is found in foods that helps to make the body strong and healthy
stages (*noun*)	the separate parts of a process

Index